A
BEAUTIFUL
VAMPIRE

By

ARABELLA KENEALY

First published in 1896

British Library Cataloguing-in-Publication Data
A catalogue record for this book is available
from the British Library

ARABELLA KENEALY

Arabella Kenealy was born in Portslade, Sussex in 1864. She was educated at home, and then at London School of Medicine for Women. After graduating, she practised medicine in London and Watford for six years, but retired in 1894 from ill health, having contracted diphtheria. Shortly before her retirement, she published her first novel, *Dr. Janet of Harley Street* (1893), and began to contribute essays to various periodicals. Over the course of her life, Kenealy published a number of other novels – including *The Love of Richard Herrick* (1902) and *An American Duchess* (1906) – and a short-story collection entitled *Dr. Smith of Queen Anne Street* (1907). Eugenicism, sexuality, and feminism feature as major themes in her work. She died of a coronary thrombosis in 1938.

I

There was a flutter indeed in the little town of Argles, when it became known that Dr Andrew had made an attempt upon the life of Lady Deverish. Andrew was a youngish, good-looking fellow, junior partner in the firm of Byrne & Andrew, the principal doctors in the place. Everybody liked him. He was as clever as he was kind. He would take equal pains to pull the ninth child of a navvy through a croup seizure as he would have done had it been heir to an earldom. Some people thought this mistaken kindness on the doctor's part – the navvy's ninth could well have been spared, especially as the navvy drank, and in any case was unable to provide properly for eight. Some went so far even as to assert that Andrew was flying in the face of Providence – to say nothing of the ratepayers – when he brought this superfluous ninth triumphantly through its fifth attack of croup. Otherwise, he was as popular as a man may be in a world wherein flaws and scandal lend to tea and bread-and-butter a stimulating quality denied to blamelessness and good repute.

'The butler says he heard raised voices,' it was whispered over dainty cups, 'and then Lady Deverish shrieked for help, and he ran in and found the doctor clutching her round the throat.'

'And only just in time. Her face was perfectly black!'

'Isn't it awful? Such a kind man as he has always seemed. Is there any madness in the family?'

'It is not certain. They say his mother was peculiar. Wrote books, and did other extraordinary things. Always wore very large hats with black feathers. Quite out of fashion, Mrs Byass tells me. She knew her.'

'What have they done with him?'

'That is the strangest part of it. She wouldn't charge

him – said it was all a mistake. So he just got into his carriage, and continued his rounds.'

'Gracious! Strangling everybody?'

'Oh, I believe not.'

'Her throat was bruised black and blue. Old Dr Byrne went at once and saw to her. He got a new nurse down from London. They say it was a nurse they quarrelled about, you know.'

'Well, they won't get anyone to believe that, my dear.'

'No, because she was as plain as could be. And Lady Deverish's groom told cook that Dr Andrew scarcely looked at her.'

'And I never heard that he admired Lady Deverish.'

'Ah! well, most men do.'

'I don't see what she wants a nurse at all for. She's the picture of health.'

'She says she suffers from nerves.'

'If all of us who suffer from "nerves" were to have trained nurses looking after us, there wouldn't be enough trained nurses to go round.'

'No, but all of us are not widows with the incomes of two rich dear departeds at our bankers, my dear.'

Now, knowing both her charming ladyship and Andrew, I was naturally interested as to why he had put hands about her beautiful throat in anything other than loving kindness. Therefore, I made a point of drinking tea with a number of amiable and gracious persons of my acquaintance during the week following this most notable attempt. All the information I got for my pains has been condensed into the foregoing gossip, and since it was insufficient for my purposes I set about seeking more. I called early at the Manor. I did not entirely credit rumour's whisper concerning the victim's mangled throat, but I knew Andrew's muscular lean hands, if he had been in earnest, would, to say the least of it, have rendered prudent her retirement for the space of some days, so that I did not expect to see anybody but her companion, Mrs Lyall.

'Gracious, how ill you look!' I could not help exclaiming, as she entered.

I had known her some months earlier as a buxom matron. Now she was a haggard old woman. Her features worked and twisted. She slid into a chair, her hands and members shaking like those of one with palsy. For several minutes she could not speak.

'You must have been sadly troubled,' I said.

She was a mild and somewhat flaccid person, one of those plump anaemic women who give one the impression that their veins run milk. But as I spoke her face became contorted. She struggled up and brandished a trembling, clenched hand.

'If he had only done it!' she cried passionately, 'if by some mercy of Providence he had only done it!'

She was transformed – distorted. It was as though some mild and milky Alderney had suddenly developed claws. She slid trembling again into her chair.

'My dear Mrs Lyall,' I remonstrated, 'if he had only done it, the world would have lost a beautiful and accomplished member of your sex – and poor Andrew's career would have come to a summary and lamentable end.'

'No jury would have convicted him,' she protested, '*not when they knew.*' She dropped her voice and searched the room with apprehensive eyes. Then she whispered, 'She is a devil.'

Now I was aware that some plain and very good women are in the habit of regarding every comely member of their sex as allied in one or another way with the Father of Evil, but it was clear that some sentiment stronger than general principles was moving Mrs Lyall.

My interest was roused. But she had come to the end of her remarks. She glanced round timorously.

'For Heaven's sake, Lord Syfret, do not mention a word of this,' she stammered. 'I am sadly unnerved. I scarcely know what I say. Poor Lady Deverish has been rather trying.' She shut her weak lips obstinately. I assured her of my discretion. I expressed sympathy, and went my way.

Byrne had nothing to tell. 'Andrew will not say a word,' he said. 'He was over-taxed. Been up several nights. She must have exasperated him somehow. Shouldn't have thought he had it in him. He has always been the kindest of fellows.'

'What does she say?'

'Laughs it off, though she don't seem amiable. Looks as if she don't want things to come out.'

'You don't mean—?'

'My dear fellow, whatsoever I mean, I do not say.'

It has always been my habit in life to take the bull by the horns whensoever circumstances have rendered this feat at the same time possible and prudent. I determined to attempt it now. Andrew, after all, was a very mild and tractable bull, despite his recent outbreak.

'I will not disguise the object of my visit,' I informed him. 'You know my weakness. Anything you tell me will go no further. The ball of Argles' scandal will get no push from me. But I like to probe human motive; and you must admit the situation is suggestive.'

He smiled – a nervous smile. I had never seen him so careworn. He shook his head. 'She has tied my hands,' he said. 'If they had let me I would have strangled her.'

'I do not wonder you are hard hit,' I adventured,

watching him. 'She is certainly a siren of the first water.'

He burst out laughing. 'Great Scott!' he said. 'Is that what they say? Do they think I am aspiring to the Deverish's hand and acres? No, no; I am not altogether a fool.'

At this moment somebody ran up the stairs and after a preliminary knock, burst into the room.

'Please, doctor, come quick,' a page-boy blurted. 'There's Lady Deverish's nurse has fallen down in the road, and they says she's dying.'

The same change came over Andrew that had come over Mrs Lyall. His face became contorted. He held a clenched fist in the air. 'Damn her!' he cried, and rushed out.

Now this ejaculation had every appearance of applying to her ladyship's nurse, and would point to an amount of callousness on Andrew's part – considering the moribund condition of that unfortunate young person – whereof I am sure he was incapable. I hasten, therefore, to inform the reader that it was intended solely and absolutely for her ladyship's bewitching self. It was as fervid and whole-souled a fulmination as I remember to have heard. It left no doubt in my mind whatsoever as to the fact of her ladyship owing her life to that timely advent of her butler. My interest was not abated. I followed Andrew out. In the next street a knot of curious persons were assembled.

'Stand back,' the doctor called as we went up. 'Give her air.'

The circle widened, disclosing the figure of a young woman in nursing dress, lying senseless on the pavement. Her upturned face was curiously pinched, though the conformation was young, and her hair fallen loose about her cheek hung in girlish rings.

'She does not look strong enough for nursing,' I remarked to Byrne, who came up at the moment.

'Strong enough,' he echoed testily. 'A week ago she was sturdy and robust. The Deverish takes care of that. Can't stand sickliness about her.' He added half to himself, 'Must be something wrong with the house. Ventilation bad or something. One after another they've gone off like this.' The girl now began to show signs of consciousness. She opened her eyes, and seeing Andrew, smiled faintly. Presently she sat up.

'When you feel equal to it, my dear,' Dr Byrne said, 'we will help you to my carriage, and you can drive straight back.'

'Back,' she repeated wildly, 'where?'

'Why, to the Manor. You must—'

She interrupted him; she caught his hand. 'No, no,' she gasped, 'not there, never there. I cannot stand another hour of it.'

'The beautiful Deverish must be something of a vixen,' I reflected, seeing the expression in the girl's face.

Andrew was helping her to her feet. 'Don't be afraid,' he said quietly, 'I will see that you do not go back.'

She looked into his face. 'What is it?' she whispered, with white lips. 'Do you know?'

'Yes, I know,' he answered, meeting her look.

I had an inspiration. Among my clientele I numbered several trained nurses. I called at the post office on my way home and wired for one. In less than two hours she was with me. I despatched her to the Manor. 'Say you have been sent from Heaven or Buckingham Palace, or any other probable and impressive source, and keep your eyes and ears open,' I enjoined her, with that utter disregard for truth and scrupulousness which I have found the greatest of all aids to me in my researches.

She returned in an hour. There was anger in her eyes. The gauze veil streaming from her bonnet fluttered manelike to the offended toss of her head.

'You did not stay long,' I said.

'My lord,' she returned, 'I did not have the opportunity. Lady Devilish – I believe you called her Devilish – just came into the room and gave a little cry, and turned her back on me as if I'd been an ogre. "Oh, you would never suit," she said, "I must have someone young" – my lord, I am twenty-six – "and plump" – I weigh ten stone – "and healthy" – I have never had a day's illness. "Send someone young, and plump, and healthy," and she marched out.'

'I suppose that would not be difficult?' I commented.

'Not at all,' she said resolutely, 'a little padding, a touch of rouge, and some minor details are all that are needed.'

'You mean to go yourself, then?'

'Yes, I mean to go,' she returned. 'If there is anything to find out she may be sorry she wasn't more civil,' she added meditatively.

'Would she not recognize you?'

I admire grit. I admired the uncompromising and superior disdain with which she met my question. She turned and left without condescending a word. In fifteen minutes she came back, or, rather, somebody did whose voice was all I recognized. Her disguise was perfect. Before, she had certainly looked neither youthful (despite her assurance as to twenty-six), nor plump (despite her boasted avoirdupois), nor healthy. Now she was plump, and young, and rosy. She had been dark; now a profusion of rich red hair rippled from her brows. I wondered why she did not always go about disguised. She explained.

'In most houses, my lord,' she said, 'there are sons, and brothers, and husbands. A woman who has her living to get by nursing can only afford to sport cherry cheeks under exceptional circumstances.'

When she had gone I dipped my pen in coloured ink and

entered her name in my diary. Whether or not she succeeded with Lady 'Devilish', she was a capable person. And capable persons are red-letter persons in a world where incompetency rules seven days out of most weeks.

II
Nurse Marian's Story

She received me with open arms. 'You are just what I want,' she said effusively. 'I loathe sickliness. There was a gaunt, haggard creature here an hour ago. Ugh!' she shuddered, 'I would not have employed her for worlds.'

I may be prejudiced, but after her remark I confess to feeling somewhat antipathetic to her ladyship. She has a curious way of staring. I suspect her of being short-sighted and shirking glasses for the sake of her looks. Certainly I have never seen anybody so brilliantly beautiful.

Upstairs I was introduced to her companion, Mrs Lyall. She did not strike me as being altogether sane. She has rather a grim smile.

'You'll soon lose those fine cheeks,' she said the moment she saw me.

'I trust not,' I returned, with some amount of confidence. (I had only just opened a new packet.) 'Is Lady Devilish rather a trying patient, then?' I asked.

She broke into a laugh. 'What did you call her?'

'I understood her name to be Devilish,' I said.

'No, it's her nature,' she retorted, looking furtively about. 'Her name has an "r" instead of an "l".'

Her ladyship was plainly no favourite of Mrs Lyall's. Indeed, everybody in the house seemed to be in mortal terror of her. The servants would not, if they could help it, enter a room where she was.

From the unhealthy faces of the household I came to the conclusion that the house was thoroughly unsanitary. I determined to investigate the drains. Whatsoever there might be that was unwholesome it did not affect the mistress. Her energy was marvellous. She never tired. When after a long day picnicking or a late ball, everybody looked as white as paper, she was as fresh and blooming and gay-spirited as possible. It seemed a mere farce for her to employ a nurse. But she had a fad about massage, and insisted on being 'massed' morning and night.

'You don't look tired,' she remarked in a puzzled way, at the end of my first night's operations. She was staring curiously at my rouged cheeks. Strangely enough I was feeling actually faint. Strong-nerved as I am, I fairly reeled.

'Whatsoever I look,' I answered her, a little irritably, 'I certainly feel more tired than I ever remember feeling.'

I thought she seemed pleased. Certainly I had said nothing to please her. No doubt she was thinking her own thoughts.

Her engagement to be married again was announced the day after my arrival. She had been already married twice. The young man – the Earl of Arlington – was, with a number of other persons, stopping in the house. He was handsome and pleasant-looking. I was told he had thrown over a girl he had cared for and who had cared for him for years in order to propose to Lady Deverish. He did not look capable of it. But, to all appearance, he was head over ears in love. He could not keep his eyes from her. He sat like a man bewitched, and neither ate nor rested.

'Poor young gentleman! He'll go the way of the others,' Mrs Plimmer, the housekeeper, confided to me.

'You don't suspect Lady Deverish of poisoning her husbands?' I returned.

'It isn't my place to suspect my betters, Nurse,' she said with dignity, 'All I say is there's something terrible mysterious. Why does everybody who comes to the Manor fail in health?'

'Drains,' I suggested.

She tossed her ample chin. 'Why did her two young husbands, as likely men as might be, sicken from the day she married them, and die consumptive? Was that drains, can you tell me?'

I thought it might have been, but having no evidence, did not commit myself.

Mrs Plimmer tossed her ample chin again, this time triumphantly. 'And why,' she proceeded, 'did Dr Andrew, as kind a gentleman as walks, try to strangle her?'

I braved her scorn and ventured 'jealousy.'

She eyed me witheringly. 'The doctor's no lady's man,' she said, 'and besides if he was, it's no reason for strangling them.'

I was unable to find any fault with the drains. I began to grow interested. I myself felt strangely out of sorts – a new experience for me.

Lord Arlington's infatuation amounted to possession. He sat staring at her in a kind of ecstasy of fascination. He was pale and moody and obviously unhappy. I was told he had lost health and spirits markedly since his engagement. Probably his conscience troubled him about the other woman. At breakfast one morning he unwrapped a little packet which had come by post for him, without, it is to be supposed, observing the handwriting. As he undid it mechanically there dropped from the wrappings a ring, a knot of ribbon, and a bundle of letters. He seemed stunned. Without a word he gathered them together and quitted the room. I met him later pacing the garden like a madman.

Poor man! His love-affair was short-lived.

A week later I was involuntary witness to a curious scene. I was sitting late one evening in the garden. Lady Deverish would not need me until bedtime, when her massage was due. Suddenly he and she, talking excitedly, came round the shrubbery.

'I have been mad,' he exclaimed, in a hoarse, passionate voice. 'For God's sake let me go free. They say her heart is broken.'

She put her two hands on his shoulders, and lifted her face to his.

'I will never let you go,' she said, with a curious ring as of metal in her voice. She wound her arms about his neck and kissed his throat. 'And you love me too much,' she added.

'Heaven only knows if it is love,' he answered, 'it seems to me like madness. I had loved her faithfully for years.'

'And now you love me, and there is no way out of it,' she whispered. She leaned up again and kissed him. Then with a little cooing laugh she left him.

He remained looking after her. 'Yes, there is one way out of it,' I heard him say slowly.

That night he shot himself.

Now, although I had known her but a fortnight, I had known her long enough to believe her superior to the weakness of being very deeply in love. Yet the night he died I was inclined to alter my opinion. He had bidden her a hasty goodbye, saying he was summoned to town. He took the last train up.

During the night I was called to her. I found her sitting up in bed, her face ashen pale, her eyes distended, her hands clasped to her head. She was gasping for breath. She seemed like one stricken; her features were picked out by deep grey lines. She did not speak, but pointed with an insistent finger to her right temple. I put my hand upon it. Then I called quickly for a light; for my fingers slipped along that which seemed to be a moist and clammy aperture, moist with a horrible, unmistakable clamminess. But when the light was brought there was neither blood nor aperture, only a curious, blanched spot, chill to the touch.

I gave her brandy, and put hot bottles in her bed. She was shaking as with ague. She clutched my hands, holding them against that ice-spot in her temple till I was sick and faint. Soon she seemed better. Some colour returned to her.

'My God, he is dead!' she said, through chattering teeth. Then she crouched down in the bed, a shuddering heap.

Next morning the news came. In that same hour he had put a bullet through his right temple. She was ill all that day, nerveless and almost pulseless. She looked ten years older. I never saw so singular a change. I sent for Dr Byrne, who attributed it to the shock of bad news. Why it developed some hours before the news arrived he did not explain. He only said: 'Tut, tut, Nurse, life is full of coincidences;' and prescribed ammonia.

Next day she was better, and suggested getting up, but changed her mind after having seen a mirror. 'Gracious!' she said, with a shudder, 'I look like an old woman.' She broke into feeble weeping. 'He ought to have thought of me,' she cried angrily.

She demanded wine and meat-juices, taking them with a curious solicitude, and carefully looking into her mirror for their effect. But she saw little there to comfort her.

'Do you think it might be my death-blow?' she questioned once through quivering lips. I shook my head. 'Ah, you don't know all,' she muttered.

In the afternoon she asked that the gardener's child

should be brought to her. He was a chubby, rosy little fellow, whom everybody petted. 'I must have something to liven me,' she said. I had never supposed her fond of children. But she held her arms hungrily for him, and strained him to her breast. Her spirits rose. Her eyes brightened: she got colour. Soon she was laughing and chatting in her accustomed manner. The child had fallen asleep, but she would not part with him. When at last she let him go, I was horrified to find him cold and pallid. He was breathing heavily, and quite unconscious. I concluded the poor little chap was sickening for something. Later, I was surprised to receive a note from Dr Andrew, whom I did not know. I dismissed him as I had done Mrs Lyall, and probably Mrs Plimmer, as not altogether sane. 'I have been called in to attend Willy Daniels,' the note ran. 'For Heaven's sake, do not let her get hold of any more children.'

Next day she was better. She seemed to have forgotten Arlington and talked only of her health. She asked again for the boy. I told her he was ill. She broke into a curious laugh which seemed uncalled for. 'Thank goodness, I haven't lost my power,' she said a minute later. But she did not explain the saying.

She was in high spirits all the morning, talking and singing and trying on new laces and bonnets. She still complained of pain in the right temple. After her massage she turned peevish, protesting that it did her no good. 'If you hadn't such a colour I should not believe you healthy,' she said crossly.

She had the parson's children to tea. It would amuse her, she said, to see them eat their strawberries. They seemed afraid of her, and eyed her from a distance. When she attempted to take the little one, it clung to me and shrieked.

But she persisted, and it soon fell asleep in her arms. On presently taking it from her, I found it chilled and breathing stertorously and quite unconscious. I thought of Dr Andrew's injunction. Heavens! what had she done? Was she a secret poisoner? I dismissed the notion forthwith. I had not left the room a moment during the time the child was with her, nor had it taken anything to eat or drink.

'What is the matter?' I demanded.

Her eye avoided mine. She answered nonchalantly: 'What does one expect? Children are everlastingly teething or over-feeding or having measles.'

Next morning I was called up at daybreak. Dr Andrew was waiting to see me. I threw on my things and went down. He was stalking up and down the drawing-room. He stared.

'You seem to have resisted her,' he muttered, looking at my cheeks. I have a long memory, and had not forgotten my rouge. He told me a wild and incredible story. He wound up by handing me a small bottle.

'Give her that dose so soon as she wakes,' he said. The man was probably a better doctor than he was an actor. His manner paraded the nature of the dose. I took out the cork and smelt it. It was as I suspected. I walked across the room and emptied its contents out of the window. 'Pardon me,' I said, 'but you are exceeding your duty.'

'Is she to be allowed to go on murdering people?' he protested. 'Do you know I have been up all night with that unfortunate baby? Do you know Willy Daniels is not yet out of danger? Good Heavens! if I am willing to take the consequences, how can one who knows the circumstances hesitate?'

'I have a safer and more justifiable plan,' I said. 'If what you say is true the remedy is simple, and poison is uncalled for. After all, Dr Andrew, your story would sound lame enough in a lawcourt. By my plan you run no risks.'

I laid it before him. He seemed interested. But he would not, after the manner of men in their dealings with women, permit me to take too much credit to myself.

'It might work,' he said lukewarmly, 'and as you say it would certainly be safer.'

I went to my room and opened a further packet of rouge. I applied it lavishly. I began to see that the health tint on my cheeks had an important bearing on the situation. I put vermilion on my lips. Then I carried my patient her breakfast.

She seemed restored and lay in her rose-pink bed, a smiling Venus. She fairly glowed with beautiful health. I thought of that poor little sick boy. 'Goodness!' I said with a start, 'how ill you look!' She ceased from smiling. She leapt across the floor, her draperies clinging round her pink flushed toes. She fled to the glass. She turned on me peevishly. 'Why did you tell me?' she protested. 'I should have thought I looked well.'

I went and stood beside her. 'Compare yourself with me.'

She was pale enough indeed by the time she had done so. 'Am I losing my power after all?' she muttered. 'Heavens! shall I grow old like other people?'

Suddenly she flung herself upon me. She pressed her lips and cheeks against my throat and face.

'Give *me* some of it,' she cried ravenously. 'You have so much vitality. Let me drain some of that rich health and colour.'

I nearly fell. It seemed as if she were actually sucking out my life. I reeled and sickened. Then with a tremendous effort I pushed her away and stumbled from the room. Was

Andrew's story indeed true? Was she a monster or merely a monomaniac?

Years ago he had said she was dying of consumption. So far as physical signs could be trusted, she had not a week to live. Suddenly she began to recover. She made flesh rapidly, gained health, and came back to life from the very jaws of death. Meanwhile, her sister, a schoolgirl, whom she insisted on having always with her, sickened and died.

Then a brother died, then her mother. By this time she had grown quite strong. Since then she had lived on the vital forces of those surrounding her. 'The law of life,' he said, 'makes creatures inter-dependent. Physical vitality is subject to physical laws of diffusion and equalisation. One person below par absorbs the nerve and life sources of healthier persons with them. Many old, debilitated subjects live on the animal forces of the cat they keep persistently in their chair, and die when it dies. Wives and husbands, sisters and brothers, friends and acquaintances: there is a constant interchange of vital force. Lady Deverish has to my knowledge been the actual cause of death of a dozen persons. Besides these she has drained the health of everybody associated with her. And in her case – a rare and extreme one – the faculty is conscious and voluntary. She was living on Arlington. The man was powerless. She paralysed his will, his mind, his energies. She robbed him of strength to resist her. The sequel is interesting, psychologically. She being for the time charged with his vitality, his sudden death, by some curious sympathy, affected her in the way you have described. She was all at once and violently bereft of the source whence she was drawing energy. But she will soon, if she be allowed, find some other to prey on. For some years I have studied her closely. She is the arch-type of a class of persons I have long had under observation. I find such power depends largely on force of will and concentration. If she can maintain these there is no reason why she should not live to be a hundred. There will always be persons of less assertive selfishness to serve as reservoirs of vital strength to her. At present her confidence is shaken, her power – therefore her life trembles in the balance. In the interests of humanity and justice she must not be allowed to regain her confidence. She lives by wholesale murder.'

III

I drank a glass of port and went back to my patient. She lay panting on her bed.

'Fie!' I said; 'that was a bit of hysteria. Come now, take your breakfast.'

She looked me in the face. A terror of death stood in beads on her skin. 'I have heard of transfusion,' she said faintly; 'if you will let me have some of the rich red blood run out of your veins into mine I will settle £500 a year on you.'

I shook my head.

'A thousand,' she said. 'Fifteen hundred.'

'I should be cheating you,' I insisted, 'even were I willing. The operation has never been really successful.'

She broke into raving and tears.

'I cannot die,' she said; 'I love life. I love being beautiful and rich; I love admiration. I must have admiration! I love my beautiful, beautiful body and the joy of life! I cannot, cannot die!'

'What nonsense!' I said. 'You are not going to die.'

'If I could only get it,' she raved, 'I would drink blood out of living bodies rather than I would die.'

An hour later she summoned the housekeeper. She had

been cogitating with a fold between her brows; her teeth set like pearls in the red of her lower lip.

'Plimmer,' she said, 'give all the servants a month's wages and an hour's notice to quit. I cannot endure their sickly faces. Get in a staff of decently healthy people. These cadaverous wretches are killing me.'

Plimmer left the room without a word. At the door she cast one look toward me and threw her hands up, as one who says: 'The Lord have mercy on us!'

I followed, and bade her stay her hand. Whether Andrew's theories were true, or whether my lady were but a person with a mania, there was no doubt but that her convictions played an important part in the case.

I threw on my things and expended a half-sovereign at the chemist's. I came back the possessor of sundry packets. These I distributed among the household with explicit directions. Her ladyship was not well; her whim must be humoured.

It is surprising what a little rouge will do. In a few minutes the servants' hall was a scene Arcadian. Even the elderly butler reverted to blooming youth. Then I said to her cheerfully:

'You are making a mistake about the servants. For my part I am struck with their healthy looks.'

'Since I have been ill?' she faltered.

She lay quiet, breathing hard through her dilated nostrils. 'Send some of them in,' she said presently.

By the time they had gone she was as white as paper. 'Good Heavens!' I heard her mutter, 'I have lost my power. I am a dead woman.'

Then she flung out her arms and wept. 'Get me healthy children,' she cried; 'I must have health about me.'

Dr Byrne, who was attending her, assented in all

innocence. 'Why, of course,' he said; 'it will be cheerful for you. Get in some cherry-cheeked children to amuse her ladyship, Nurse.'

I nodded – in token that I was not deaf – not at all in acquiescence. Food and wine I supplied in plenty, but neither children nor adults. I isolated her *in toto*. I allowed her maids only to come near her long enough to dust and arrange the room. I have seen her fix them with a basilisk stare, straining her will. She had undoubtedly some baleful hypnotic power which set them trembling and stumbling about in curious, aimless fashion. They would seem drawn, as by some spell, to stand motionless and dazed beside her bed. Then I would turn them face about and parading their roseate tints, scold them for idleness and dismiss them. She would stare after them in a despair which, under other circumstances, would have been pitiful. The sense that her power was gone robbed her actually of power. She raved and cursed her self-murdered lover for involving her in his death.

Whether Dr Andrew and I were justified in that we did I sometimes wonder now. Then I had no room for doubt. In face of the horrible facts it did not occur to me to question it. If that she believed were true, we were assuredly justified; if not, that we did could not affect results.

Andrew's theory of those results is that she had lived so long on human energy that food in the crude state stood her in little stead. Certainly, though she was fed unremittingly on the choicest and most nourishing of diets, she was an aged and haggard woman in a week. Nobody would have recognized her. She shrivelled and shrank like one cholera-stricken. One day her dog stole into the room. She put out her hand and clutched it voraciously. I took it an hour later from her. It was dead and stiff.

How I myself, and a nurse I had called in to help me, kept life in us I cannot say. I had been an abstainer. Now I drank wine like water. All round her bed was an atmosphere as of a vault, though outside it was sunny June.

She raged like one possessed. 'You are murdering, murdering me,' she cried incessantly.

Dr Byrne thought her mind wandering. I knew it centred with a monstrous, selfish sanity. He sent for one of the first London consultants. After a lengthy investigation the great man pronounced her suffering from some obscure nervous disease. 'Nothing to be done,' he said. 'I give her three days: most interesting case. Hope you will succeed in getting a *post mortem.*'

Once she fixed me with her baleful eyes, how baleful was seen now that their fine lustre and the bloom beneath them were gone.

'I have had ten years more of life and pleasure than my due,' she chuckled in her shrivelled throat – the throat now of an old, old woman.

Then she broke into dry-eyed crying. 'I thought I could have lived another ten.' She begged once for a mirror. I thank Heaven that with all my heat of indignation against her, I was not guilty of that cruelty.

Dr Andrew called daily for my bulletin. Everything science afforded in the way of food and stimulant, he scrupulously got down from London.

'We must give her every chance,' he said, 'every justifiable chance, that is.'

After a few days I was again single-handed. My nurse-colleague succumbed. I felt my powers failing. I could scarcely drag about. I prayed Providence for strength to last so long as she should. Even in the moment of dissolution, such was her frenzied greed of life, that I believed should some non-resistant person take my place, she would struggle back to health.

Once when I arranged her pillows, she seized my hand, and before I could withdraw it she had carried it to her mouth and bitten into it. I felt her suck the blood voraciously. She cried out and struck at me as I wrenched it away.

She died in the third week of her isolation. I saw the death change come into her shrivelled face. Then in the moment wherein life left her she made one supremest effort.

It seemed as though my heart stopped. My head took on my chest, my hands dropped at my side. Then I swayed and fell headlong across her bed. They found me later lying on her corpse. I am convinced that had she been a moment earlier, had she nerved her powers the instant before, rather than on the instant life was leaving her, she would be alive to this day, and I— As it was, I did not leave my bed for a month.

'If I were to write that story in the *Lancet*,' Dr Andrew said, 'I should be the laughing-stock of the profession. Yet it is the very key-note of human health and human disease, this interchange of vital force which goes on continually between individuals. Such rapacity and greed as the Deverish's are, fortunately, rare; but there are a score such vampires in this very town, vampires in lesser degree. When A. talks with me ten minutes I feel ten years older. It takes me an hour to bring my nerve-power up to par again. People call him a bore. In reality he is a rapacious egotist hungrily absorbing the life-force of anyone with whom he comes into relation – in other words, a human vampire.'

www.ingramcontent.com/pod-product-compliance
Lightning Source LLC
Chambersburg PA
CBHW030532260626
47157CB00005B/2001